Properties for Sale

· BACHELOR PAD · · ·

...all but sophisticated ...rrow close to nightclubs!

XCLUSIVITY ND SECURITY!

...his spacious burrow is protected ...a state-of-the-art briar patch. ...ound-the-clock security ...rovided by Br'er Bear, Inc.

EGG-CELENT BURROW

How sweet it is —modern burrow located next to chocolate factory. ...ree on-site egg-decorating and ...asket-weaving classes in spring.

FOREST OASIS

Old log burrow, just right for a thumpin' good time— invite all your friends to visit. Communal living, ideal for skunks, moles, and rabbits.

EXTRA-LARGE BURROW

So spacious that even a six-foot tall rabbit will feel invisible! Available exclusively through Harvey Realty.

STREAMSIDE

Burrow for Summer Sublet An easy hop to water's edge!

LUXURY BURROW /ESTATE SALE

Previously owned by single dragon for eons. A gem! Bring your architect!

Under the Rowan Tree

Hillside den near fairy p... ...fo... pied-à-... pixies, ...and oth...

WHAT WILL YOU BUIL...

Pristine meadow available lots of acreage, great ... large family compound. Predator-free neighborhood.

Medieval-style

Burrow, nicely situated in front of the Cave of Caerbannog.

Modern Burrow ★★ with ★★ Dream Kitchen

A must for foodies! Store your carrot tops and root vegetables in the spacious pantry and create delicious meals in this chef's kitchen.

DUPLEX BURROW

Spacious two-story burrow available for rent. Two levels with separate exits from each story.

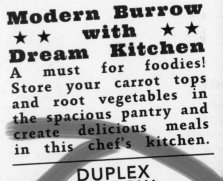

...NER'S DELIGHT

...your own in this ...us burrow with a ...sunny back garden. ...d in the presti- ...Hundred Acre Wood.

WINTER FUN!

Weekend rental Cozy 2-chamber burrow slopeside Quick hop to all snow sports. Arctic hare-approved

LIGHT

A Tale of Rabbit Real Estate

POW!

BROOKLYN, NY

Gregory and Petunia Bunny
are looking for a new home.

A burrow
to call
their own.

**The fairies next door
are too loud.**

Our bunny babies
will never get any sleep.

**Look at all these rubies
in the dragon's hoard!**

This place is
too expensive.

Steve Light is a teacher, artist, and storyteller whose many children's books include *Trains Go, Trucks Go, Diggers Go, Planes Go,* and *Boats Go; Have You Seen My Dragon?* and *Have You Seen My Monster?* Steve lives in New York City. See more of Steve's work at stevelightart.com.

Properties for Sale or Rent

Never Be Late Again!

...ight in the heart of Won-...erland, close to everything. ...omes fully furnished with ...ooking glass and tea set.

Fixer Upper Old barn.

Needs work. Close to friendly farm. Weasels need not apply.

5-CARROT LOCATION! ★★★★★

Nice burrow with easy commute to car-rot farm. Great views.

Quiet Burrow for Rent

Dug deep and spacious, with lots of closets and built-in shelves—great for families!

MUSICIANS' DELIGHT!

Great deep-woods location; attached toadstool studio—practice with your band! Songbirds especially welcome, but no badgers, please.

CAVE AVAILABLE

Underground living at its best. Entrance below water. A humid paradise. NO FEE.

EH, WHAT'S UP? A fabulous bunny burrow, that's what! Make a left toin at Albukoikee. Free hunting season license with purchase. No ducks, please!

BUNNY DREAM HOME

Charming and spacious family burrow under a shady oak tree. Move-in ready!

HIGH-STYLE LIVIN'

Upper-branch nest, feather-lined and lux-urious. Tree-top views!

DAM FINE!

Newly renovated beaver lodge, right on the water! Constructed from highest quality beaver-cut logs.

A Burrow Like No Other!

New construction-6 different living levels, all with dirt floors and root ceilings! No ants—mole friendly neighborhood.

WEASEL PARADISE

COMPLEX UNDER NEW MANAGEMENT! FORMER CHIPMUNK BURROW BENEATH OLD ROCK PILE. SLEEPS 10!

Shady Pine Tree Burrow

Smells great all year long! Free pine cones with purchase

MUD-ALICIOUS! ECO-FRIENDLY

SWAMP BURROW MADE OF BEST QUALITY ORGANIC MUD

Farm Living

A burrow you wouldn't lose your coat over. Close to McGregor's Farm